wee words for wee ones

presents

Two Truths

and a

FIB

Poetry Anthology

A Poetic Introduction to 30 Subjects with a T W I S T

edited and compiled by

Bridget Magee

**I dedicate this book to my two TRUE loves,
Joe, Co, Mo and Smidgey-oh!**
(I FIB you not, math is not my strong suit. ;)

ISBN: 978-1-7373303-5-6

wee words for wee ones
Zug, CH

www.bridgetmagee.com

Table of Contents

Dear Reader,

As a teacher, I start each term by playing the ice-breaker game, "Two Truths and a Lie". (Game: introductions made by telling three tidbits about yourself, two truths and a lie. The other people playing try to guess which of the three tidbits is the lie.) It is a fun, creative way to introduce ourselves and to build community.

On New Year's Day 2022. I noticed that 2023 will start off just like the Fibonacci Sequence 1.1.23. (Yes, I like to plan that far ahead! *ahem*.) I thought to myself, *wouldn't it be fun to create a poetry anthology that introduces various subjects, a wide variety of poetry forms and amazing poets based on this ice-breaker game with a tie-in to math?*

Things *spiraled* into motion until they coalesced into the **Two Truths and a FIB Poetry Anthology** that you are holding in your hands right now.

On the following pages you will be poetically introduced to 30 subjects by 29 amazingly talented poets. Each subject will have **two poems** that are **true** (written in the poetry form of the poet's choosing) and **one poem** that is not true, a **FIB** (written in the **Fib poetry form***.) The FIB poem will have a corresponding **Fact Check** to set the record straight. Then the poets will share the **Poetry Forms** they used to create their truth poems. Finally the poets will introduce themselves *Two Truths and a FIB style*. Between each poetic section, you will find small examples of the Fibonacci sequence in everyday life. Math is all around us.

But as my dedication illustrates, math *sum*-times doesn't *add* up for me. Another thing that doesn't *add* up is when people fib. Fibs tend to *multiply*, spiraling out of control...
Again, math is all around us!

My hope, dear reader, is that you learn something new, try your hand at a poetry form brilliantly illustrated on these pages, and ultimately, that you see the world around you through a Fibonacci lens. (But stick to the truth, it's less head spinney...)

xo, Bridget

*****Fib**: a 6-line poem with the syllable count 1, 1, 2, 3, 5, 8 created by Gregory K. Pincus

fern leaves

Two Truths and a FIB about...

Ants

Truth #1

Dig, dig, dig the soil
tunnel to the nest
eagerly, busily, carefully, hurriedly
work for the colony's best.

Truth #2

Some little ants
got in my pants
I couldn't get them out.

I tried to wiggle,
I tried to jiggle,
but ants stayed in my pants.

They tickled my knees
They are such a tease
Oh please, I think I am going
to
    sne
        ee
          eee
            ZE!

The ants are gone,
scattered on the lawn.
Beware the crawling critters.

Ants
king
of pets
fetching balls
running, playing chase
best friend to snuggle at night time.

©2023, Kathleen Mazurowski

Fact Check:

Ant live in colonies with one queen. Most ants are under 1/2 inch in length. Ants can not fetch balls or snuggle with people.

Poetry Forms:

Truth #1: Parody

- imitation of a particular style of a well known work
- based on the nursery rhyme, *Row Row Row Your Boat*

Truth #2: Tercet

- multiple- three lined stanzas poems that rhyme in various ways
- this poem has 4 stanzas:

AAB

CCD

EEE

FFG

Introducing the Poet...

Kathleen Mazurowski

Kathleen Mazurowski's first full time teaching job required an "about me" interview which she wrote/performed as a poem. (Thanks to Shel Silverstein and Jimmy Jet for the inspiration.) She's been an extra in *Chicago Med*, *Chicago PD* and *Chicago Fire* television shows. And she loves to travel and has visited all 50 of the United States and many other countries.

Which statement about Kathleen is a FIB?
Turn to the "Poet Fact Check" section at the back of the book to find out!

pine cone

Two Truths and
a FIB about...

Blood
Suckers

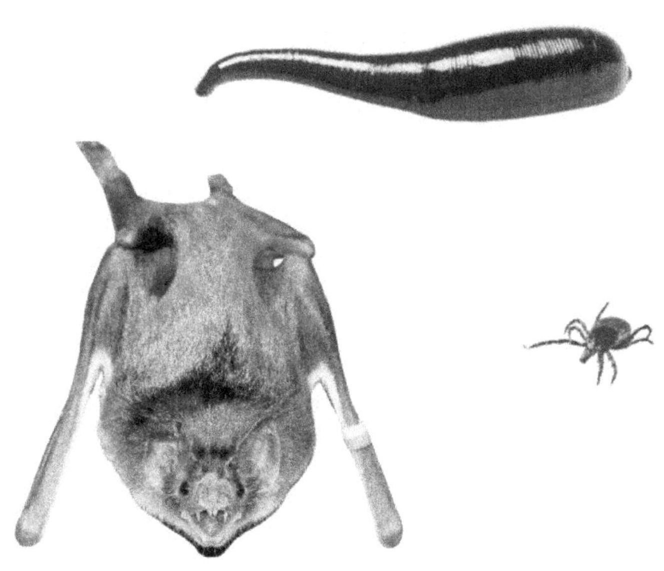

Truth #1

        Leeches,
       leeches
      lurk near
      beaches,
       rippling
        through
        the reeds
          and mud.
          Leeches,
           leeches
           don't eat
            peaches,
           leeches
             seek to
              siphon
               blood.

Truth #2

Ticks don't tick, nor do they click,
or buzz and whirr or chrip-chirp-chirp,
in fact, they make no sound at all.
No bigger than an apple seed,
they creep in hush amongst the brush
in hopes to latch their eight wee legs
onto an unsuspecting lunch.

Their menu's jammed with juicy meals
like rabbit, rodent, dog and deer,
but any boy or girl will do.
No, ticks don't tick, nor do they click
or buzz and whirr or chirp-chirp-chirp,
but if they make a sound at all
perhaps it would be *slurp-slurp-slurp*.

They
scre ee e ech . . .
at *DAWN*.
Plump with blood,
vampire bats *wing* home,
li tt e r i ng caves with human Bone.

©2023, William Peery

Fact Check:

Vampire bats generally dine on livestock such as cattle and pigs, but rarely humans. They are the only mammals that feed, not suck, entirely on blood. The amount is so small, maybe two tablespoons, the host often doesn't even notice. These little bats do not kill their hosts, let alone litter caves with human bones. The bite, however, can result in the transmission of a disease such as rabies.

Poetry Forms:

Truth #1: **Monometer Concrete Poem**

- monometer refers to a line of verse that is only one metrical foot in length
- these lines are quite short - generally just one or two words long with a single stressed syllable
- the rhythm created by monometer is rather distinctive and fun to read
- concrete poetry, often referred to as "shape poetry," is poetry whose appearance on the page expresses meaning beyond the written words to further enhance the poem
- in this poem, the layout of text, or shape of the poem, hints at a leech - did you notice it?

Truth #2: **Blank Verse**

- verse refers to poetry whose words form a metrical pattern of stressed and unstressed syllables
- in this poem, the stressed and unstressed syllables alternate
- the first two lines with the stressed syllables in bold:
    Ticks don't **tick**, nor do they **click**,
    or **buzz** and **whirr** or **chirp-chirp-chirp**,
- did you notice that every line also has a pattern of four stressed syllables, or four metrical feet?
- can you pick out the stressed syllables in the rest of the poem?
- the reason we call this poem "blank" verse is because there is no end rhyme, or at least not a pattern of end rhyme

Introducing the Poet...

William Peery

Residing in the bone-dry hills of Southern California, you might find William Peery writing, gardening, watching superhero movies with his wife and children, or perhaps hunting for rattlesnakes. Many years ago, he notably played electric guitar on two songs for the Beatles. Additionally, William once finished an Ironman triathlon under twelve hours and has even solved a Rubik's cube in one breath.

Which statement about William is a FIB?
Turn to the "Poet Fact Check" section at the back of the book to find out!

nautilus sea shell

Two Truths and a FIB about...

Bubbles

Photo credit: Kim Douillard

Truth #1

Birds wake up
dawn
in melodic
tunes
throwing tweets on air:
bubbles floating from a bubble wand

©2023, Margaret Simon

Truth #2

Blow soap suds
Up with a straw
Billowing, bouncing,
Building hexagons
Light-bending
Effervescence rising

©2023, Margaret Simon

Blow
Big
Sturdy
Flexible
Shape-shifting whispers
Large enough for you to ride on.

©2023, Margaret Simon

Fact Check:

Bubbles blown from a soapy mixture are all in the shape of a sphere. They do not change shape. They are fragile, so even the slight tap of a finger can pop them. Certainly no chance for riding on.

Poetry Forms:

Truth #1: **Pi-Ku 3.14159**

- a form taken from the mathematical term *pi*.
- follows a syllable sequence that matches the mathematical term: 3.14159

Truth #2: **Acrostic**

- uses a striking word, in this case, BUBBLE
- the first word of each line begins with a letter from the striking word

Introducing the Poet...

Margaret Simon

Margaret Simon lives near a bayou (like a river) and enjoys canoeing when the opportunity arises. She has three daughters and 4 grandchildren. She teaches only fifth graders.

Which statement about Margaret is a FIB?
Turn to the "Poet Fact Check" section at the back of the book to find out!

plant

Two Truths and
a FIB about...

Cats

Its tail
is a multi-tasking masterpiece
a counterbalance
to avoid catastrophes
a communication aid
even a cozy scarf
for a cool night
A categorically
elegant appendage

It has a set of whiskers
its very own measuring tape
to estimate narrow spaces
and make a quick escape!

soft
pawed
night-time
wanderer
sleek shadow-stalker
stealing the breath of sleeping babes

©2023, Molly Hogan

Fact Check:

No, cats do not steal or suck the breath from sleeping infants. This myth may have started because cats are attracted to the warmth of sleeping babies or because cats have a bad reputation for hanging out with witches.

Poetry Forms:

Truth #1: Free Verse

- no set form
- no set meter
- no set rhyme scheme
- kind of like a cat :)

Truth #2: Quatrain

- 4 lines
- ABCB rhyme scheme

Introducing the Poet...

Molly Hogan

Molly Hogan lives in a 220 year old farmhouse in Maine and loves to drive her tractor around her property. She once helped her 400 pound pig, Daisy, deliver seven piglets...on Labor Day! And she once lived on a 43-foot sailboat and sailed from Maine to the Bahamas.

Which statement about Molly is a FIB?
Turn to the "Poet Fact Check" section at the back of the book to find out!

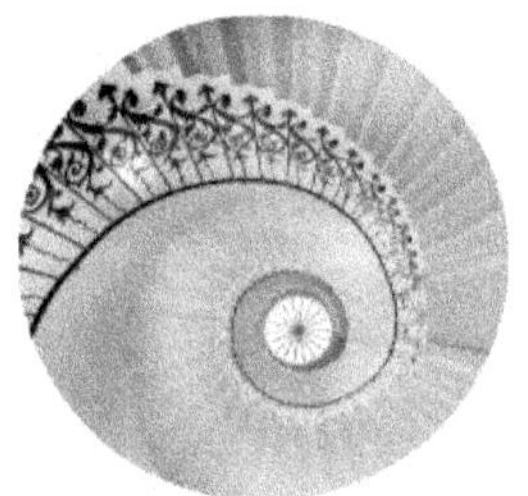

spiral staircase

Two Truths and a FIB about...

Chickens

Truth #1

When you're low in the order of pecking,
you're assigned to the duties of checking.
At the end of your perch
your objective's to search
for those predators ripe for the wrecking.

Where the wisdom of nature comes through,
you're designed with a brain split in two.
As each eye works alone
observations have shown,
you can survey and sleep while you do.

Though you're dealt with the bottom-most card,
there will soon be a changing of guard.
When you move from your keep
you will then get to sleep
like the hens held in higher regard!

Truth #2

Though toothless, I'm an omnivore.
I munch on veggies, grubs and more,
as well as pebbles, sand or grit -
all swallowed with a coat of spit.

While still intact, it makes a stop
to wait inside my storage crop
until the stomach calls it in
to let the breaking down begin.

My gizzard's muscles, much like teeth,
then mash and grind what's sent beneath.
And when the bits are finely ground
the lot of it's intestine-bound.

More
sun
means less
production
when it comes to hens.
On longer days, the less they lay.

©2023, Colleen Murphy

Fact Check:

Naturally, for hens, less sunlight means less egg production. As the days grow shorter hens lay fewer eggs (unless artificial light is used).

Poetry Forms:

Truth #1: **Limericks**

- each stanza consists of five lines
- AABBA rhyme scheme
- lines 1, 2 and 5 have three stressed syllables
- lines 3 and 4 have two
- often humorous

Truth #2: **Rhyming Quatrains**

- three four line stanzas
- AABB rhyme scheme
- iambic tetrameter (four feet with each foot consisting of one unstressed followed by a stressed syllable)

Introducing the Poet...

Colleen Murphy

Colleen Murphy lived on a farm and showed horses in her youth. She now raises free range, egg-laying chickens. She has been writing poetry since the age of five.

Which statement about Colleen is a FIB?
Turn to the "Poet Fact Check" section at the back of the book to find out!

cut out of nautilus sea shell

Two Truths and a FIB about...

Cows

Truth #1

Can the label "sporty" fit
an even-toed ungulate?

These hooved mammals
showcase skills
two-toeing it on
fields and hills.

Truth #2

Cows bound
after balls that bounce
and nudge them with a nose -
or pounce.

Cows run fast -
17 mph and faster.
(They'd beat you
racing through
the pasture.)

Cows can swim -
they're buoyantly designed.
(And don't wear floaties
as we're inclined.)

We
all
know cows
are stellar
competitors in
vaulting - of the celestial kind.

©2023, Joan Riordan

Fact Check:

A dog might indeed laugh if a cow jumped over the moon but bovines are earthbound and do not jump over celestial bodies.

Poetry Forms:

Truth #1: Question and Answer Poem

- first two lines (a couplet) ask a question
- AA rhyme scheme
- last four lines (a quatrain) answer the question
- BCDC rhyme scheme

Truth #2: Offset Poem

- em dashes used to insert pauses, add emphasis
- parentheses used to add to a thought
- ABCB rhyme scheme

Introducing the Poet...

Joan Riordan

Joan Riordan is an educator with decades of experience. She enjoys baking, taking long walks and making butter and ice cream from the milk of her own cows. She is the co-author of the teacher resource book, *Doing Language Arts in Morning Meeting.*

Which statement about Joan is a FIB?
Turn to the "Poet Fact Check" section at the back of the book to find out!

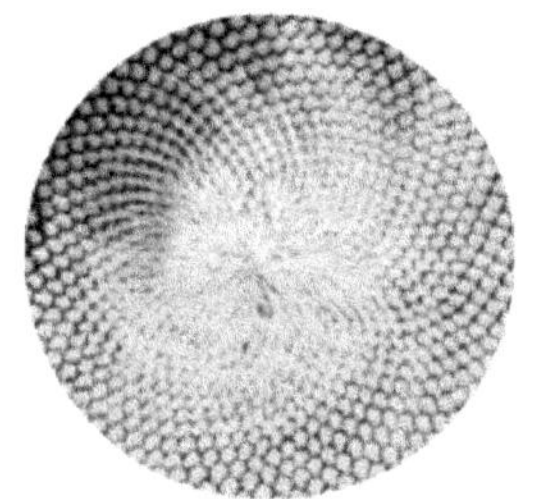

Gerbera daisy

Two Truths and a FIB about...

Eleven and Seven

Did you know eleven and seven
are odd numbers that are also even?
As words, they are always **even**
at the end.

©2023, Karuna Mistry

Did you know eleven and seven
are odd numbers that are also even?
When combined they make an **even**
eighteen.

©2023, Karuna Mistry

```
odd
plus
even
appears odd
but always even
a property of addition
```

©2023, Karuna Mistry

This FIB states one of the properties of addition incorrectly. The correct property of addition is: odd number plus even number always equals an odd number. Therefore, the FIB poem is a fib.

Poetry Forms:

Truth #1: **Observation Poem**

- opens with the phrase "Did you know..."
- points out an unexpected observation
- makes reader see the world in a new way

Truth #2: **Observation Poem**

- opens with the phrase "Did you know..."
- points out an unexpected observation
- makes reader see the world in a new way

Introducing the Poet...

Karuna Mistry

Karuna Mistry is a maths teacher. He is also a drawing artist. And he knows how to play chess.

Which statement about Karuna is a FIB?
Turn to the "Poet Fact Check" section at the back of the book to find out!

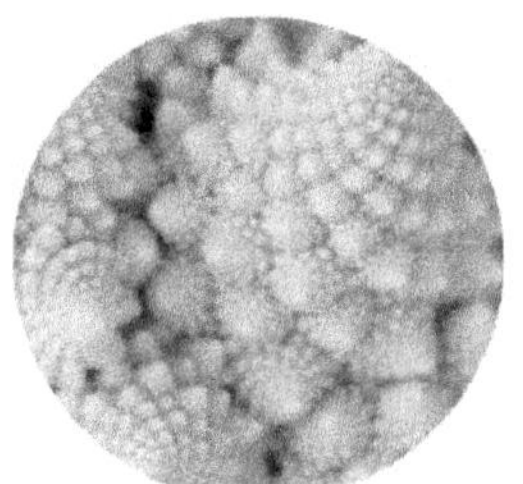

Roman cauliflower

Two Truths and a FIB about...

Eyes

Truth #1

Short-horned lizards possess a great trait --
when threatened they simply inflate.
The predator soon
leaves the spiky balloon
to search for some easier bait.

But some predators still want to try.
So, the lizard shoots blood from its eye.
Up to five feet away
the unpleasant spray
compels them to quickly say, "Bye!"

Truth #2

I think that you might be surprised
to find when comparing features
that ostrich eyes are super-sized --
the largest of all land creatures.

Though others simply cannot match
those big eyeballs, there is a catch --
their eyes are bigger than their brain!
If they knew that, would they complain?

All
bats
are blind
and must use
echolocation
for successful navigation.

Fact Check:

It is true that many bats that hunt at night use echolocation. As the high-pitched sounds they make bounce off of objects, they are better able to navigate in the dark. BUT bats are not blind. They can see. Echolocation is a useful method to helps bats determine the size and speed of food sources and other things within 55 feet (17 meters). If an object is further away, the bat relies on eyesight. Also, some bats (like the fruit bat) don't use echolocation at all. Instead, they depend on their good sense of vision to locate food.

Poetry Forms:

Truth #1: **Double Limerick**

- two stanzas, each a limerick
- each limerick is five lines
- lines 1, 2, and 5 have three metrical feet
- lines 3 and 4 have two feet
- rhyme scheme: AABBA

Truth #2: **Rispetto**

- a poem in an octave, made up of 2 quatrains
- most often written in iambic tetrameter
- OR it can be syllabic with lines between 8 and 12 syllables
- rhyme scheme is ababccdd or abababcc or abab cddc
- this poem is syllabic with 8 syllables in each line and follows the ababccdd pattern

Introducing the Poet...

Linda Hofke

Linda Hofke has lived in three different countries. Her days are spent working on a farm and her nights writing poetry. Caramel always makes her cough.

Which statement about Linda is a FIB?
Turn to the "Poet Fact Check" section at the back of the book to find out!

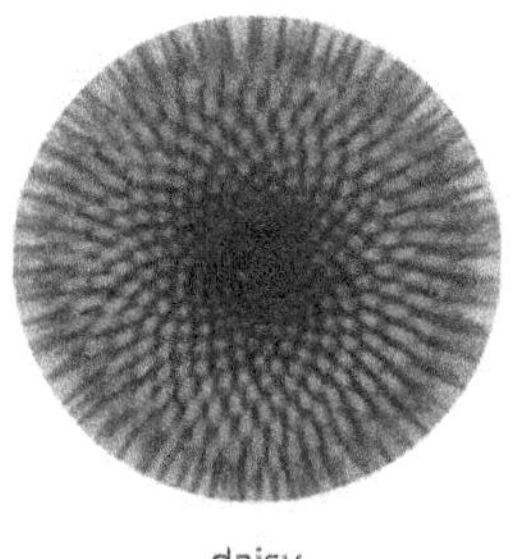

daisy

Two Truths and a FIB about...

a Flower Garden

Spring surprises -
purple globe of blossom
on a tall slender stalk -
Allium,
onion's cousin,
spicing up the garden.

©2023, Mary Lee Hahn

In my garden
native plants abound;
volunteers are welcome,
are not
said to be weeds. Case
in point - Fleabane. I
value its darling fringed flowers and
embrace its polkadots of joy.

©2023, Mary Lee Hahn

My
whole
garden
is burning!
The Red Hot Fire Poker
sparked the blaze; Prairie Smoke smolders.

©2023, Mary Lee Hahn

Fact Check:

Red Hot Fire Poker and Prairie Smoke are plant
names. They do not literally burn.

Poetry Forms:

Truth #1: **Free Verse**

- this poem uses alliteration and assonance as the primary poetic devices

Truth #2: **Acrostic**

- the letters in the vertically-written word "invasive" begin the first word in each line of the poem
- each line elaborates on the idea of "invasive"

Introducing the Poet...

Mary Lee Hahn

Mary Lee Hahn has been a teacher for more than half of her life. Out of all the plants in her gardens, more than half are herbs. More than half of her hobbies involve making something.

Which statement about Mary Lee is a FIB?
Turn to the "Poet Fact Check" section at the back of the book to find out!

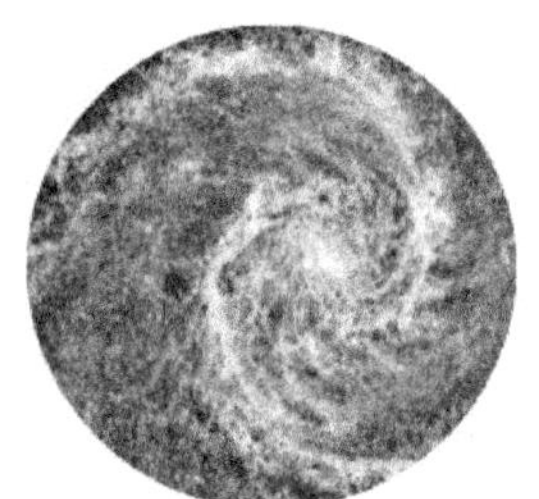

spiral galaxy

Two Truths and a FIB about...

George Washington

Truth #1

On Christmas night the moon shone bright and spread a silver glow
Upon my men and 60 boats that waited down below
To cross the icy waters of the mighty Delaware
And fight the troops in Trenton that were singing carols there.

The cargo boats from Durham works were built to carry ore:
Tonight they carried men and horses to the other shore.
Through snow and sleet and biting wind my soldiers poled those boats
With Henry Knox directing them in loud stentorian notes.

The waves beat ice and flotsam up against their sturdy sides,
And of those crossing not a single one forgot these rides.
For, after we had won a battle that would change the war,
Each boat would cross the Delaware just like it did before.

And so, until I'm old and gray, I'll have this tale to share,
Of how my cannons, men, and horses crossed the Delaware.

Truth #2

Five deadly years had passed since when we crossed the Delaware
And with our Continental Army gave the Brits a scare –
Five years in which we fought and bled and bravely took a stand
For freedom from colonial rule to reign throughout this land.

The French had joined our cause and sent their warships from the south.
They sailed into the Chesapeake and quickly blocked its mouth.
When we arrived we used their cannons to bombard the town:
Two weeks of that and their defenses started coming down.

The Brits surrendered, we took Yorktown, and it came to be
That my Virginia victory sealed the war and made us free.

I
did
not turn
twenty-one
when we adopted
that Gregorian calendar.

Fact Check:

The Gregorian calendar was introduced by Great
Britain - and thus the colonies - in September 1752.
Great Britain was actually fairly late in adopting the
Gregorian calendar. Most Catholic countries went
first, then continental Europe. When adopting the
Gregorian system an adjustment of 11 days had to be
erased from the calendar. The next country to adopt
the Gregorian calendar after Great Britain was
Sweden the following year in 1753. If George had been
a Swede, he would have missed his 21st birthday on
February 22nd because the Swedes erased the 11 days
between February 17 and March 1.

Poetry Forms:

Truth #1: **Ballad**

- the core structure for a ballad is a quatrain
- this poem deviates slightly with three quatrains and one couplet
- the rhyme scheme is:

  AABB

  CCDD

  EEFF

  GG

- written in iambic heptameter
- tells a story - in this case of an event

Truth #2: **Ballad**

- the core structure for a ballad is a quatrain
- this poem deviates slightly with two quatrains and one couplet
- the rhyme scheme is:

  AABB

  CCDD

  EE

- written in iambic heptameter
- tells a story - in this case of an event

Introducing the Poet...

Stephan Stücklin

Stephan Stücklin is a Swiss-US dual national who grew up in Switzerland around the time the country introduced daylight saving time. He works in a steel mill where he heads up the laboratory. In his free time, he enjoys playing Frisbee golf and spending time with his wife and four dogs.

Which statement about Stephan is a FIB?
Turn to the "Poet Fact Check" section at the back of the book to find out!

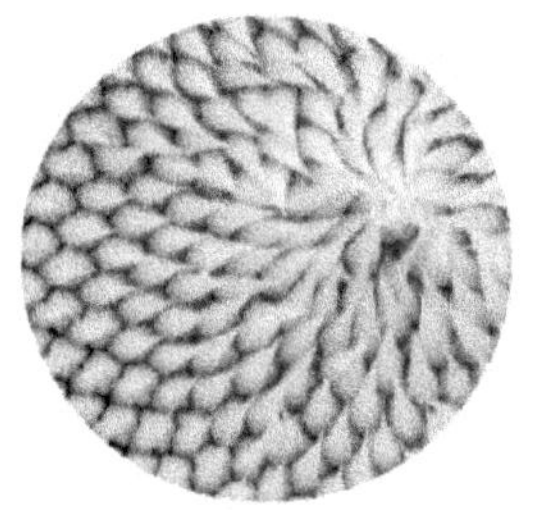

sunflower

Two Truths and a FIB about... Greta Thunberg

Truth #1

An island of plastic gassing the sea:
Greta saw what we didn't want to see
        she saw the fever she felt the heat
like she saw CO_2 with her naked eye
her brain the kind that cannot lie
            silence became strike
                    fear became a red-hot ire

Truth #2

Get real, world! The science can't be
refuted. Our house is on fire; it's an
emergency that we can't wait
to answer. How dare you
adults pretend that everything is fine?!

"She's
just
a teen-
aged girl who
can't stop climate change.
She'll never make a difference."

Fact Check:

As I write this in 2022, Greta Thunberg is still just a teenaged girl aged 19. But the idea that she could not make a difference, couldn't help to stop climate change, is an enormous fib. Greta's School Strikes for Climate caught the world's attention, and her fiery refusal to allow adult excuses made her TIME Magazine's youngest Person of the Year in 2019. We are all paying better attention to our future because of Greta.

Poetry Forms:

Truth #1: **Free Verse**

- employs poetic elements like assonance, rhyme and rhythm according to the poet's choice
- may have a visible structure or pattern invented just for this particular poem

Truth #2: **Acrostic**

- the first letters of each line spell a word or name
- in this case, the words is the name of the subject of the poem

Introducing the Poet...

Heidi Mordhorst

Heidi Mordhorst has been writing poetry since she was 5; her first poem was about rain. She performed for several years with an LGBTQ salsa dancing performance team. And she is the owner of one dozen cats, all named after ice cream flavors.

Which statement about Heidi is a FIB?
Turn to the "Poet Fact Check" section at the back of the book to find out!

staircase

Two Truths and
a FIB about...

Hippopotamus

Truth #1

Because I have such fragile skin,
I like to spend all day wet.
I see water, and dive right in,
because I have such fragile skin.
When dry, a sun block will begin
to ooze from me like sweat...and yet
because I have such fragile skin,
I like to spend all day wet.

Truth #2

Because I'm round, weighing even more than cars,
Folks underestimate my sprinting pace.
While not a famous lanky running star,
I'd beat you if you challenged me to race.

Because I eat plants, and resist all meat,
Folks underestimate my massive might.
My teeth grow longer than a human's feet,
With force that's stronger than a lion's bite.

Because I'm cute (now don't you disagree),
Folks underestimate how mad I get.
If people stand between my calf and me,
I'll then attack for real - not fake a threat.

So if you see a hippo, give a cheer,
Don't underestimate - and don't go near!

```
Deep,
deep
water
is the best
for me to swim in.
I've no need to touch the bottom.
```

©2023, Cynthia L. Greene

While hippos can stay under water for 5 minutes, they don't actually swim, but rather propel themselves off the bottom.

Poetry Forms:

Truth #1: **Triolet**

- eight-lined poem with two rhymes
- the first line is repeated as lines 4 and 7
- the second line is repeated as line 8
- the rhyme scheme is ABaAabAB (capital letters are repeated lines)

Truth #2: **Shakespearean Sonnet**

- a fourteen-line poem written in iambic pentameter
- the syllables of the lines read: dah-DUM dah-DUM dah-DUM dah-DUM dah-DUM
- the lines are organized in three stanzas of four lines each followed by a couplet (group of two lines)
- the rhyme scheme is:

ABAB

CDCD

EFEF

GG

Introducing the Poet...

Cynthia L. Greene

One of Cynthia L. Greene's favorite foods is olives. She loves to dress up in costumes. And she's accustomed to getting up early.

Which statement about Cynthia is a FIB?
Turn to the "Poet Fact Check" section at the back of the book to find out!

Cephalopod

Two Truths and a FIB about...

a Housefly

Slower than a dragonfly but faster than a mosquito,
a humble housefly streaks by clocking five miles per hour,
swiftly buzzing past the angry baker waving a flyswatter.

©2023, Lill Pluta

The fly's wings
beat two hundred times
per second,
sounding tones
along the F major scale,
music from nature.

©2023, Lill Pluta

Poor
fly
escapes
being squashed
but like all flies, dies
in two dozen, too short hours.

©2023, Lill Pluta

Fact Check:

On average, adult houseflies live 15 - 25 days. If they
are lucky, they might make it to the ripe old age of
two months.

Poetry Forms:

Truth #1: **Sijo**

- the Korean sijo is comprised of 3 lines
- each line has 14-16 syllables
- the complete poem contains a total of 44 to 46 syllables
- sijo is related to tanka and haiku
- originally, sijo poems were created to be songs

Truth #2: **Shadorma**

- the shadorma has six lines
- the syllable counts are 3/5/3/3/7/5
- it can have many stanzas as long as each follows the syllable pattern
- there is no set rhyme scheme

Introducing the Poet...

Lill Pluta

Lill Pluta is an avid fan of sumo wrestling. When she isn't watching sumo, she can be seen kite surfing over local beaches. However, her favorite sport is writing poetry.

Which statement about Lill is a FIB?
Turn to the "Poet Fact Check" section at the back of the book to find out!

plant growing

Two Truths and a FIB about...

Ice

Truth #1

The dull, white sky is still.
Sounds are softened,
frosted fingers, frozen inside mittens
pointing: *Look!*

Above the door, with glassy tendrils
grasping the ledge, they hang: icy sentinels poised,
pointing back at winter's sculptures:
mirrored puddles cracked in jagged patterns,
glazed webs of glacial lace stretched across the hedges.

Ethereal adornments - transfixing, yet transient,
like icicles in the morning
dripping,
        drip
            drip

                    gone.

©2023, Claire Schlinkert

Truth #2

I am melting tears of sorrow,
while you're frozen in inaction.
With no time, nor hope, to borrow,
I am melting tears of sorrow.
For the lives destroyed tomorrow
through Earth's burning chain reaction,
I am melting tears of sorrow,
while you're frozen in inaction.

©2023, Claire Schlinkert

Trains
made
of ice,
with chilled-out
passengers, snake through
Germany at glacial pace. *Brrrrrrr!*

©2023, Claire Schlinkert

Fact Check:

Whilst German ICE trains do exist, they are fast trains, not slow or cold ones, and certainly not made of ice! Here, ICE is an acronym, standing for Inter-City Express.

Poetry Forms:

Truth #1: **Free Verse**

- the lines are free of any rules around rhythm or rhyme scheme

Truth #2: **Triolet**

- has eight lines
- the first line is repeated in lines four and seven
- the second line is repeated in line eight
- lines three and five rhyme with line one
- line six rhymes with line two
- the triolet poetic form is thought to have originated in France in the 13th century

Introducing the Poet...

Claire Schlinkert

Claire Schlinkert is a British children's poet, who has published her poetry online, and in magazines and anthologies; several of her poems have been commended/ highly commended in recent children's poetry competitions. When she's not playing with words, she enjoys singing in a choir, going on family outings, meeting friends for tea and cake, and occasionally ballroom dancing round the house when nobody's looking. She is currently learning how to ride a unicycle, whilst simultaneously juggling tangerines.

Which statement about Claire is a FIB?
Turn to the "Poet Fact Check" section at the back of the book to find out!

gardenia flower

Two Truths and
a FIB about...

Ice Cream

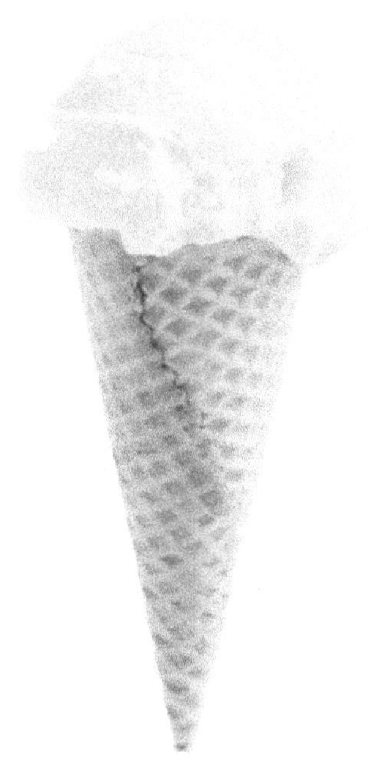

Truth #1

```
Ice cream,
Summer shiver,
Change jingling in pocket.
Kids jostle for the ice cream truck.
Chill out.
```


Truth #2

```
Machine's
Quick twisty top --
Showy new invention.
No more, "3 scoops of strawberry!"
New day!
```

Gramps
Says,
"Milking
when freezing
creates a quick serve
Vanilla ice cream treat."
©2023, Linda Baie

Fact Check:

Grandfathers give good advice, don't they? In below-zero temperatures, couldn't a child be persuaded to milk if he or she was told Old Clara would give him or her a "frosty"? No, this isn't true. Farmers give their cows warm and dry bedding plus more food because when cows digest their food, the fermentation creates heat, keeping them warm in low temperatures. Their udders do not begin to freeze and give Frosty treats, but instead, keep giving milk. Grandfather lied!

Poetry Forms:

Truth #1: **Cinquain**

- poems are five lines long
- 2 syllables in the first line
- 4 syllables in the second line
- 6 syllables in the third line
- 8 syllables in the fourth line
- 2 syllables in the fifth line
- can be rhymed or unrhymed

Truth #2: **Cinquain**

- poems are five lines long
- 2 syllables in the first line
- 4 syllables in the second line
- 6 syllables in the third line
- 8 syllables in the fourth line
- 2 syllables in the fifth line
- can be rhymed or unrhymed

Introducing the Poet...

Linda Baie

Linda Baie played trombone in high school and college bands. After moving to Colorado, she became an avid skier. She owned a horse named Silver at her grandparent's home when she was a kid; as an adult, she continued riding her Arab mare named Mariah housed at a nearby horse farm.

Which statement about Linda is a FIB?
Turn to the "Poet Fact Check" section at the back of the book to find out!

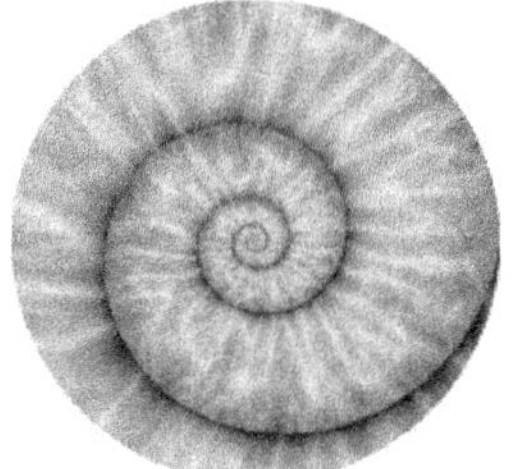

mollusk

Two Truths and
a FIB about...

Kindergarten

Truth #1

dressed in style
one backpack
two pigtails

one school bus
from daycare
to new school

back and forth
home at six
whew, long day!

©2023, Carol Varsalona

Truth #2

My new life as a Kinder starts now.
Excited but I hope we play.
Mommy wants photos. Say cheese!
"Dad, drive to daycare, please."
Eat then on the bus.
Must adjust to
no stuffies.
Day ends.
Tired.

©2023, Carol Varsalona

New
school
adds up
to no fun,
no friends, no playtime.
Kindergarten is not for me.

©2023, Carol Varsalona

Kindergarten is a new experience for children but it is fun with creative learning and play.

Poetry Forms:

Truth #1: **Tricube Poem**

- a mathematical form invented by Phillip Larrea
- each stanza contains three lines
- each poem contains three stanzas
- no rules for rhymes, meter, etc. -just three, three, and three

Truth #2: **Nonet Poem**

- a nine-line poem
- each line contains specific, descending counts
- the first line contains nine syllables, the second line contains eight, the third line contains seven, and so on
- the last line of nonet poetry contains one syllable

Introducing the Poet...

Carol Varsalona

Carol Varsalona is a retired educator and consultant. She is a creative writer known on social media for her educational experience in English language arts and as a published poet and blogger. In addition, Carol's passion is creating, curating, and publishing digital seasonal galleries of artistic expressions on social media.

Which statement about Carol is a FIB?
Turn to the "Poet Fact Check" section at the back of the book to find out!

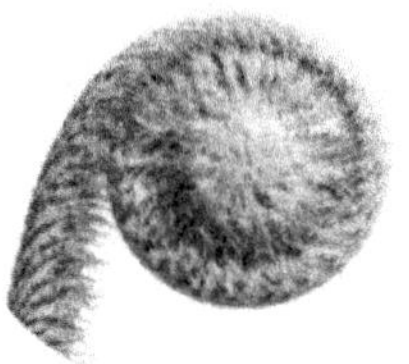

fern frond

Two Truths and a FIB about...

Libraries

Truth #1

When I need a sense of peace, I walk
into my library. Here is order. Books of all kinds
suit me and everyone, really. Keyboards
click softly. In an office behind the
big desk, a pot of coffee brews. Someone's earbuds
turned up loud -- like summer insects.
Big breath in; breath back out. I let my eyes
travel shelves of book spines.

forest of old trees
stories sorted into groves
nothing I need more

©2023, Linda Mitchell

Truth #2

Mom, mom, MOM! Drop me off here.
It's OK. I'll walk the rest. I've opened the door
before our car rolls to a stop, my Switch case
swings after me as Mom calls out,
Bye! Ten o'clock! Don't Forget.
All the tables in the YA section are full
by the time I arrive. SonicSpyder is already fist bumping
KweenKool in the graphic novel corner. I'm just in
time for the first round of my library game night tournament.

library game night
teen warriors in battle
conquer flashing screens

©2023, Linda Mitchell

old
still
silent
library
a place of the past
no one enters them anymore

©2023, Linda Mitchell

Fact Check:

Many people who are not familiar with libraries imagine that they are quiet places of silence. I've seen adults shush young people who are enjoying the wonders of books, DVDs, puzzles, games, and programmed events...which is silly! Today's libraries in schools and out in the public realm are vibrant places of reading and so much more! Have you seen maker spaces at libraries? How about a magic show or a model train demonstration? Libraries are not quiet, dead spaces. They are full of the excitement and sounds of learning.

Poetry Forms:

Truth #1: **Haibun**

- a haibun is a short prose poem followed by a haiku (sometimes a tanka)
- the prose poem consists of sensory images using descriptive language
- the haiku (or tanka) is meant to reinforce OR contrast the prose poem

Truth #2: **Haibun**

- a haibun is a short prose poem followed by a haiku (sometimes a tanka)
- the prose poem consists of sensory images using descriptive language
- the haiku (or tanka) is meant to reinforce OR contrast the prose poem

Introducing the Poet...

Linda Mitchell

Linda Mitchell is a poet, school librarian, and lion tamer. One of these is her day job, one is her passion and the third is her dream! She loves to write early in the mornings before anyone except her pet lion, Ira, is up; it's when she gets her best ideas and words.

Which statement about Linda is a FIB?
Turn to the "Poet Fact Check" section at the back of the book to find out!

agave plant

Two Truths and a FIB about...

Lightning

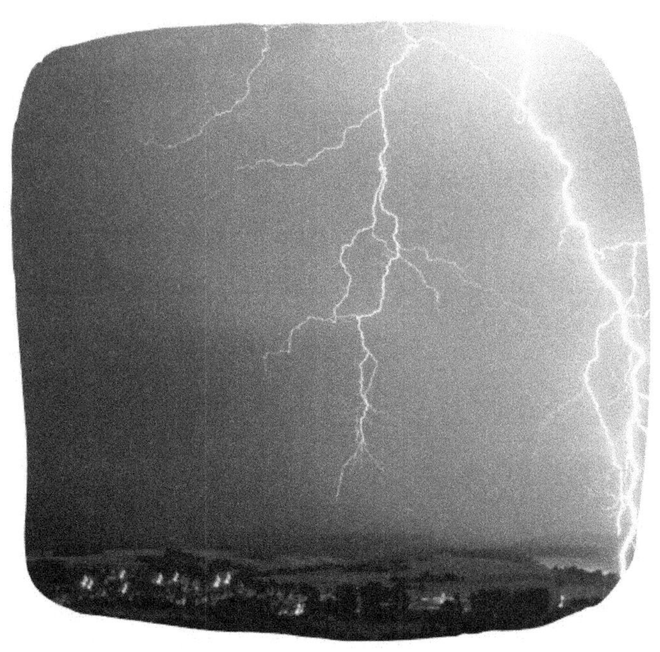

Truth #1

Lightning dances in the sky,
mesmerizing from up high.
To the beat of its own drums,
lightning comes then says goodbye.

Truth #2

Ice colliding in the clouds.
Charges separating.
Electrons flowing to the ground.
Lightning's captivating.

Pressure rising from the heat.
Air expanding fast.
Sonic shock waves traveling.
Thunder's heard at last.

Crack!
Boom!
Lightning.
No worries.
I've been struck before.
It never strikes the same place twice.

©2023, Tricia Torrible

Fact Check:

Lightning can, and often will, hit the same place twice. In fact, the Empire State Building gets struck by lightning each year between 25 and 100 times!

Poetry Forms:

Truth #1: **Englyn Cyrch**

- Welsh form
- contains any number of quatrains (4-line stanzas)
- each line contains 7 syllables
- the last syllables of lines 1, 2, and 4 rhyme with each other
- the last syllable of line 3 rhymes with the second, third, or fourth syllable of line 4

Truth #2: **Ballad Quatrains**

- 4-line stanzas
- ABCB rhyme scheme
- lines 1 and 3 use iambic tetrameter (4 beats per line)
- lines 2 and 4 use iambic trimeter (3 beats per line)

Introducing the Poet...

Tricia Torrible

Tricia Torrible has been an avid writer since childhood and now enjoys writing books and poetry for children. She lives in North Carolina, USA with her family, where she also enjoys hiking, drinking green tea, and finding an absurd amount of four-leaf clovers. Contrary to what her FIB poem may suggest, she has never been struck by lightning, but she has dodged a pitchfork that was hurled toward her from a tornado!

Which statement about Tricia is a FIB?
Turn to the "Poet Fact Check" section at the back of the book to find out!

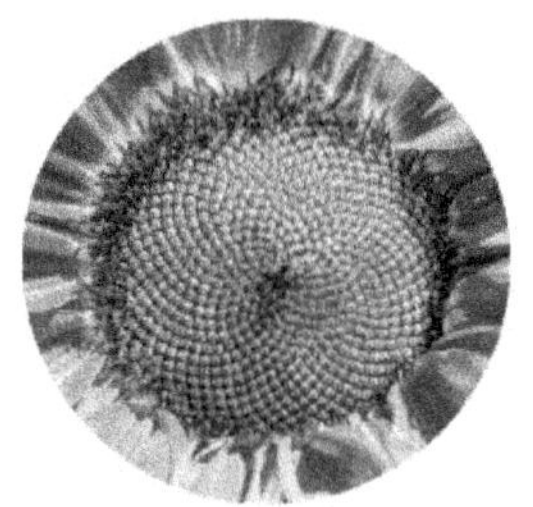

sunflower

Two Truths and
a FIB about...

Mars

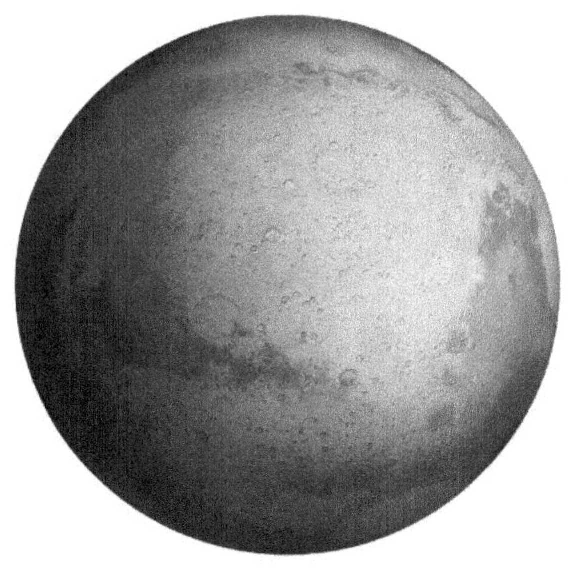

Our neighbor is covered in dust
the color of iron-rich rust.
But scientists bet
it used to be wet
and water's still trapped in the crust!

©2023, Lisa Varchol Perron

Anchored in orbit
around our shared star, and yet
spilling into space.

©2023, Lisa Varchol Perron

Footnote: Mars lost its strong magnetic field and thick atmosphere long ago, and therefore some of its air and water has escaped into space.

```
Hot,
lush,
stormless.
Oxygen
and gardens abound.
Perfect for a Sunday picnic.
```

©2023, Lisa Varchol Perron

Fact Check:

Mars is cold, dusty, and windy—the opposite of what this poem describes. Mars has very little atmosphere, and you would need to bring your own oxygen to breathe. Humans have not yet visited Mars, but it took the rover Perseverance seven months to arrive. (It's definitely not a leisurely day trip!)

Poetry Forms:

Truth #1: **Limerick**

- five lines, usually with anapestic meter
- lines 1, 2, and 5 have three metrical feet
- lines 3 and 4 have two feet
- rhyme scheme: AABBA

Truth #2: **Haiku**

- three nonrhyming lines
- lines 1 and 3 have five syllables
- line 2 has seven syllables
- often contains an image of a moment in time

Introducing the Poet...

Lisa Varchol Perron

Photo credit: Carter Hasegawa

Lisa Varchol Perron loves to travel, especially by train. Some of Lisa's favorite childhood memories are from her time spent at Space Camp. Lisa once flew through the air on a bicycle.

Which statement about Lisa is a FIB?
Turn to the "Poet Fact Check" section at the back of the book to find out!

mollusk

Two Truths and
a FIB about...

Mathematics

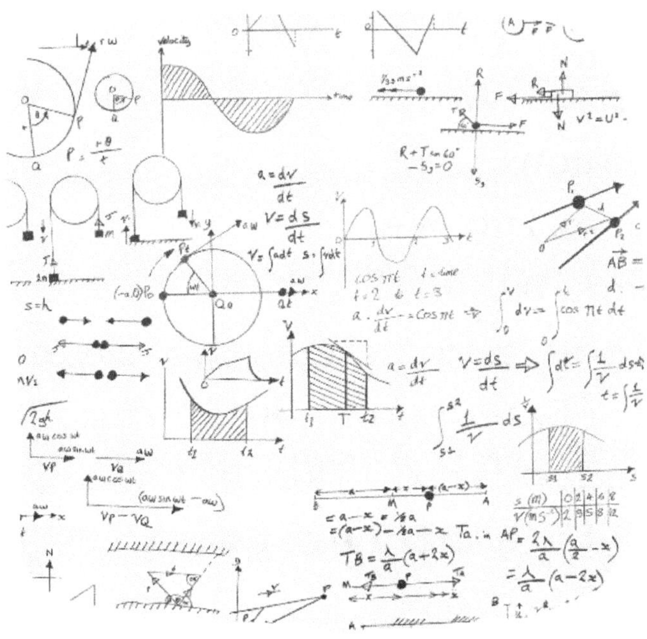

Truth #1

Zero. Resting place.
From this absence, numerals
grow and radiate!

Truth #2

Two times two.
Such potential!
Ever growing --
exponential.
Two times two times two once more.
Eight! (Expanding out from four.)
Keep ascending like a tower,
rising to a higher power.

No
such
thing as
negative
on a number line!
(What an outrageous suggestion.)

© 2023, Heather Kinser

Fact Check:

In fact, there IS such a thing as "negative numbers"! On a number line these values are shown as extending out to the left of zero and are represented as having negative signs in front of them. But these negative signs do not indicate subtraction. Negative numbers are the opposites of their "positive number" counterparts and are useful for representing certain types of values, such as temperatures below freezing (in the metric system) or money that has been borrowed.

Poetry Forms:

Truth #1: Haiku

- a Japanese poetic form
- three un-rhymed poetic lines
- usually takes the form of 5 syllables, 7 syllables, 5 syllables
- a simple yet thoughtful observation about life and nature

Truth #2: Sestain

- a 6-line rhyming poem (that can vary in rhyme scheme and meter)
- AABBCC rhyme scheme
- trochaic tetrameter (although the first two lines here are broken, for effect)

Introducing the Poet...

# Heather Kinser

Heather Kinser is a poet and picture book author who writes about microscopes, rock formations, caves, and earwax. She resides in the San Francisco Bay Area, under a majestic redwood tree. You can learn more about Heather and her books at HeatherKinser.com.

Which statement about Heather is a FIB?
Turn to the "Poet Fact Check" section at the back of the book to find out!

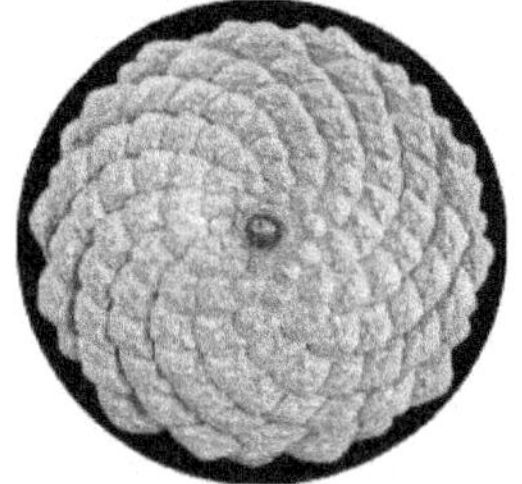

pinecone

Two Truths and
a FIB about...
Monarch
Butterflies

Like soft sparks of magic
    swoop effortlessly through air.

Flit-flutter by milkweed
    laying tiny eggs there.

My heart breaks imagining
    them vanishing everywhere.

©2023, Michelle Kogan

Milkweed and monarchs—two peas in a pod,
grow
together
during
summer,
grow
flower
pollinate
eggs.
Grow
monarchs and milkweed—two peas in a pod.

©2023, Michelle Kogan

Bee,
bird,
hmmm, who?
Only two
insects love milkweed,
monarchs and their caterpillars.

©2023, Michelle Kogan

Fact Check:

While it's true that monarch butterflies and their caterpillars both love milkweed, there are many more than just two insects that love milkweed. Other insects that love milkweed include: a whole suite of butterflies, wasps, bees, and beetles.

Poetry Forms:

Truth #1: **Three-stanza Couplet**

- stanzas in poetry are groupings of lines together to form a unit
- stanzas help the reader's eye while also forming shape, space, sense, and story
- a couplet is made up of two lines
- this poem is composed with two lines in each of the three stanzas
- the second line of each stanza rhymes

Truth #2: **Skinny Poem**

- Truth Thomas created the Skinny poetry form
- it has eleven lines
- the first and eleventh line use the same words though they can be rearranged, and shorter is better
- the second through tenth lines have one word per line
- the second, sixth, and tenth lines repeat the same word
- Skinny try to convey a "vivid image" in very few words
- they can be about anything

Introducing the Poet...

Michelle Kogan

Michelle Kogan ponders petals, beauty, nature and humanity as a poet, writer, artist, and instructor. Her poems are published in many children and adult anthologies. She's so captivated with her creative endeavors that she rarely sleeps.

Which statement about Michelle is a FIB?
Turn to the "Poet Fact Check" section at the back of the book to find out!

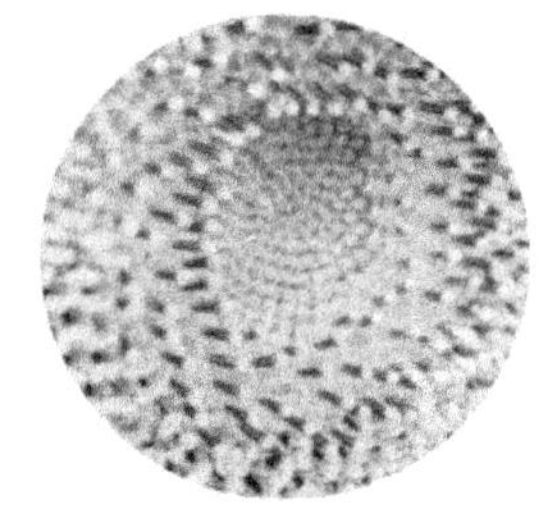

sunflower

Two Truths and
a FIB about...

the Moon

the long-night moon makes me curious,
hypnotized with wonder and awe
as it lights the garden path,
paints shadows in the grass --
a luminary
in the dark sky,
our faithful
cosmic
friend

from
darkness
a tiny
crescent appears,
spreading over time,
waxing to half a dime,
creeping farther and farther
reaching, stretching toward the edge
until finally it lights the night --
fully illuminated, glowing, bright

old
man
in the
moon safeguards
creatures of the night
until sun's bright light dawns the day

©2023, Rose Cappelli

Some of the moon's features that we see from Earth appear as light and dark patches. They are often interpreted as the face of a man, especially in the Northern Hemisphere, where people have created stories to explain the man in the moon.

Poetry Forms:

Truth #1: **Nonet**

- nine-line poem
- first line has nine syllables
- each succeeding line decreases by one syllable
- can be rhymed or unrhymed

Truth #2: **Etheree**

- ten –line poem
- each line increases in syllable count from one to ten
- named for its creator, Etheree Taylor Armstrong
- can be rhymed or unrhymed

Introducing the Poet...

Rose Cappelli

Rose Cappelli is a former reading specialist who taught reading and writing to students from Kindergarten to high school for many years. Rose enjoys spending time writing picture books and poetry in addition to skiing and snowboarding. She lives in Chester County, PA with her husband and rescue dog, Cyrus.

Which statement about Rose is a FIB?
Turn to the "Poet Fact Check" section at the back of the book to find out!

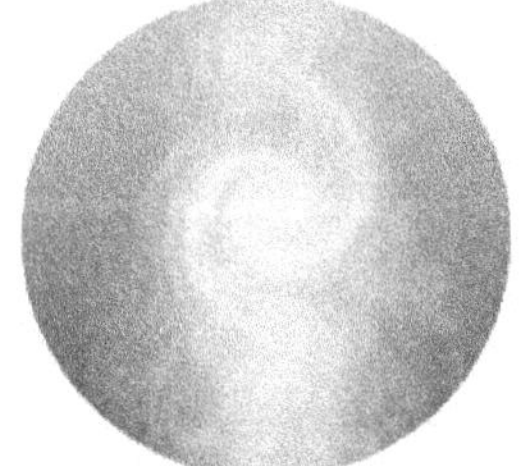

smoke pattern

Two Truths and a FIB about...

the Nose Knows

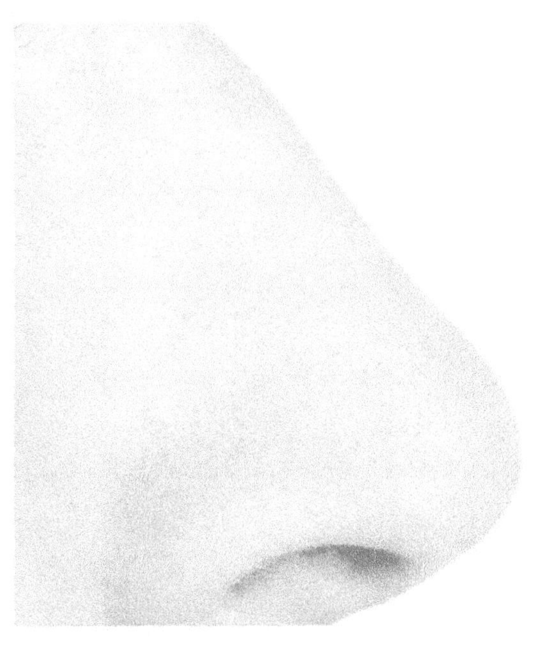

Truth #1

Thermographic cameras measure heat
and blood flow to the body and the brain.
Scientists now use this tech to map
emotions like surprise or fear or pain.

When a person lies, the nose is key.
It heats up so the camera can detect
when fibbing is afoot -- the brightest hues
light up the nose, so lies don't go unchecked.

Truth #2

Trickily, Dickily
Nixon the President
lies about Watergate
break-ins--the cheat.

Downfall would hasten if,
pre-futuristically,
scientists knew to test
Nixon's nose heat.

Lie
and
your nose
grows and grows
l-o-n-g, l-o-n-g-e-r, l--o--n--g--e--r--
a honker like Pinocchio's.

© 2023, Helen Kemp Zax

Blood rushes to people's noses when they lie. Liars' noses heat up and, therefore, light up thermographic cameras. Noses do not grow longer like Pinocchio's, however, when people fib.

Poetry Forms:

Truth #1: **Rhyming Quatrain**

- two 4-lined stanzas
- ABCB rhyme scheme
- most lines iambic pentameter
- most lines ten syllables
- each unstressed syllable is followed by a stressed syllable

Truth #2: **Double Dactyl**

- a dactyl is a three-syllable word
- first accented syllable is followed by two unaccented ones
- two quatrains
- two dactyls in each line
- first line is usually funny or made-up, rhyming dactyls like "higgledy-piggledy"
- lines 4 and 8 consist of one dactyl with an extra accented syllable
- lines 4 and 8 rhyme
- line 6 or 7 is a one-word double dactyl
- poem is humorous

Introducing the Poet...

Helen Kemp Zax

A former teacher and lawyer, Helen Kemp Zax spends her days writing poetry that has won prizes from Hunger Mountain and YorkMix and has appeared in many anthologies and magazines. She lives in Washington, DC with a view of the United States Capitol from her apartment. Her writing companion is a crazy Aussiedoodle named Huckleberry Finn, who has a pet stuffed dog named Tom Sawyer.

Which statement about Helen is a FIB?
Turn to the "Poet Fact Check" section at the back of the book to find out!

gemstone spiral

Two Truths and
a FIB about...

One

Counting one to ten
is the same as adding one
to zero ten times.

One eighth of a pizza is
an ooey-gooey slice.
One twelfth of a birthday cake
makes eating twice as nice.

A fifty-second of a deck's
a single playing card.
A hundredth of a football field
is three feet or a yard.

A thousandth of ten-dollar bills
still leaves you with a cent.
A fraction of a day with math
is always time well spent.

Don't
try
to learn
addition
because one and one
is two, but also...eleven.

©2023, Kelly Conroy

You absolutely SHOULD learn addition (and subtraction, and multiplication, and geometry, and calculus...)! Math is fun and consistent and amazing. One plus one is ALWAYS two. Two ones next to each other ALWAYS make eleven. The word "and" is the troublemaker in this FIB poem.

Poetry Forms:

Truth #1: **Haiku**

- first and third lines have 5 syllables
- second line has 7 syllables
- does not rhyme

Truth #2: **Rhyming Quatrain**

- three 4-lined stanzas
- ABCB rhyme scheme
- every other syllable is stressed

Introducing the Poet...

Kelly Conroy

Kelly Conroy's favorite story is Peter Pan. Her favorite subject was Reading. She lives with her husband, two sons, and mini goldendoodle near Pittsburgh, PA, USA.

Which statement about Kelly is a FIB?
Turn to the "Poet Fact Check" section at the back of the book to find out!

staircase

Two Truths and a FIB about...

Opossums

Opossum hunts down rats and voles
and garden beetles, snails, and slugs;
she gobbles rattlesnakes and moles
and cockroaches -- such tasty bugs.

She feasts on roadkill, rotten eggs,
and funky fruit that folks have trashed.
While others scorn such waste and dregs,
Opossum's proudly unabashed.

While 'Possum lacks gourmet cachet,
these rancid snacks keep her alive.
What's more, she's got a role to play:
she helps the ecosystem thrive!

©2023, Christy Mihaly

Huffalump, puffalump,
'Possums (*Didelphis*), if
threatened, may show off their
bared teeth, and hiss.

Facing real danger, they'll
characteristically
conk out, emitting a
stench you can't miss!

©2023, Christy Mihaly

We
must
protect
our livestock
from the rampages
of predatory opossums.

The scruffy-looking Virginia opossum, *Didelphis virginiana*, does not go on rampages. Rather than preying on livestock, opossums eat garbage, insects, and other unsavory things. Though they may look scary when they bare their teeth and snarl, they're harmless, and if seriously threatened, will "play 'possum," freezing as if dead, until the danger passes.

Poetry Forms:

Truth #1: **Rhyming Quatrain**

- three quatrains (4-lined stanzas)
- rhyme scheme: ABAB

Truth #2: **Double Dactyl**

- a form of light verse invented by Paul Pascal and Anthony Hecht in 1951.
- eight lines arranged in 2 quatrains, each consisting of 3 double-dactyl lines plus a line consisting of a dactyl plus a single syllable. (A dactyl consists of three syllables, one stressed followed by two unstressed, as in "elephant." Logically, a double-dactyl line contains two dactyls!)
- the two single syllables (last word of each stanza) rhyme.
- line 1 must be a nonsense phrase, such as "higgledy-piggledy".
- line 2 is the subject of the poem and should be a proper name (such as "Benjamin Harrison"), though in the Opossum poem, this is slightly fudged – because poets get to play around with the rules sometimes.
- line 6 should be a single double-dactylic word, here: "characteristically".

Introducing the Poet...

Christy Mihaly

Christy Mihaly left a successful career as a lawyer in order to write books and poems for children. She often wishes she had become a sea captain instead. Christy lives in Vermont, where in her spare time she walks in the woods looking for opossums, and plays the cello (though not simultaneously).

Which statement about Christy is a FIB?
Turn to the "Poet Fact Check" section at the back of the book to find out!

nautilus sea shell

Two Truths and
a FIB about...

Owls

Fluffy white owlet
snuggled in blanket of down -
beak hungry for meat.

Your screech's ladder
sounds fair warning across night
until silent flight.

An
owl's
wise eyes
mesmerize,
spiral hypnotize -
Fibonacci-ize. And prey dies.

©2023, Jennifer Raudenbush

Fact Check:

Owls' wide eyes may look hypnotic, but they can't actually hypnotize other animals or human beings.

Poetry Forms:

Truth #1: **Haiku**

- a short form of poetry that originated in Japan.
- it's characterized by 17 syllables: 5 in first line, 7 in second line, and 5 in third line
- traditionally, haiku are image-based and nature-themed
- more modern forms tackle almost any subject
- the third line typically features an observation or surprise

Truth #2: **Haiku**

- a short form of poetry that originated in Japan.
- it's characterized by 17 syllables: 5 in first line, 7 in second line, and 5 in third line
- traditionally, haiku are image-based and nature-themed
- more modern forms tackle almost any subject
- the third line typically features an observation or surprise

Introducing the Poet...

# Jennifer Raudenbush

Jennifer Raudenbush lives with her husband, teenage son, and West Highland white terrier in eastern Pennsylvania, where its natural beauty provides endless inspiration. She loves to cuddle with cats, adventure with family, and escape with books. Jen writes picture books, middle grade novels, and poetry, and is agented by Natascha Morris at the Tobias Literary Agency.

Which statement about Jennifer is a FIB?
Turn to the "Poet Fact Check" section at the back of the book to find out!

Broccoflower

Two Truths and a FIB about...

Snakes

Garden snake lingers
absorbing morning sunlight
solar powered

©2023, Molly Hogan

Every so often its
Cloak of patterned scales
Doesn't quite fit.
Yielding to necessity
Snake gradually sloughs
Its skin in its entirety.
Such a neat trick!

©2023, Molly Hogan

Look
out!
Supple
snake uses
two unblinking eyes
to hypnotize and transfix prey.

©2023, Molly Hogan

Fact Check:

Snakes do not hypnotize their prey. The myth might be due to the fact that snakes lack eyelids, so they have an unblinking stare. Also, sometimes their prey will freeze when sensing the snake's presence, which might make them appear hypnotized.

Poetry Forms:

Truth #1: Haiku

- 3 lines
- typically no more than 17 syllables
- focus on nature
- includes a season word
- non-rhyming

Truth #2: Acrostic

- a certain letter of each line in the poem, when combined with the others, spells a word
- in this poem the word is ECDYSIS
- most often it's the first letter of each line

Introducing the Poet...

Molly Hogan

Throughout her life, Molly Hogan has had a variety of jobs. She was a professional pastry chef for many years. She also once worked at a bank in Hamburg, Germany. Finally, she was an extra in the movie Jumanji.

Which statement about Molly is a FIB?
Turn to the "Poet Fact Check" section at the back of the book to find out!

spiral staircase

Two Truths and
a FIB about...

Spring

Truth #1

Spring slips in
     breathless
     late as usual
          with no apology,
     trailing her ragged green robe,
               smudged with mud and
               laced with snow
                    behind her,
     a shawl of fog draped
          upon her tangled curls.
With a basket of dandelions
   looped across her arm,
she blinks her violet eyes
          smiles
and sips morning dew from cups of tulips.

Truth #2

                    tiny
               packages
          carefully wrapped
     plain or polka dotted
     blue satin or creamy silk
     one crackles and splinters
     as the surprise inside
          pokes its slick beak
          and silky head up
               to say hello

Sham!
Snowed
by Spring's
tulip breath,
we shrugged off sweaters,
mittens...adrift in deception.

©2023, Karla Wendelin

Fact Check:

Spring IS the Fib! Unlike the swagger of Summer, whoosh of Winter, sassy dance of Autumn, Spring saunters in, making us think we can stash the winter gear...until we wake up one morning shivering and see tulip cups filled with snow.

Poetry Forms:

Truth #1: **Free Verse**

- no strict meter or rhyme scheme
- no prescribed number of lines or line length
- reflects the natural cadence of speech

Truth #2: **Concrete Poem**

- also known as a "shape poem"
- words are arranged in a shape that depicts the subject of the poem
- number of lines, line length, meter, and use of poetic devices relate to the intended shape

Introducing the Poet...

Karla Wendelin

Karla Wendelin is a lover of trees, birds, art museums, and animals who smile, all of which inspire her poetry and picture books. When Karla writes, a poem generally comes quickly as she sits at her computer and types it straightaway knowing that she can revise it later. She enjoys helping students find their poetic voice and sharing techniques with teachers in classrooms on her website, www.prairiesunshine.net/poetrystudio/.

Which statement about Karla is a FIB?
Turn to the "Poet Fact Check" section at the back of the book to find out!

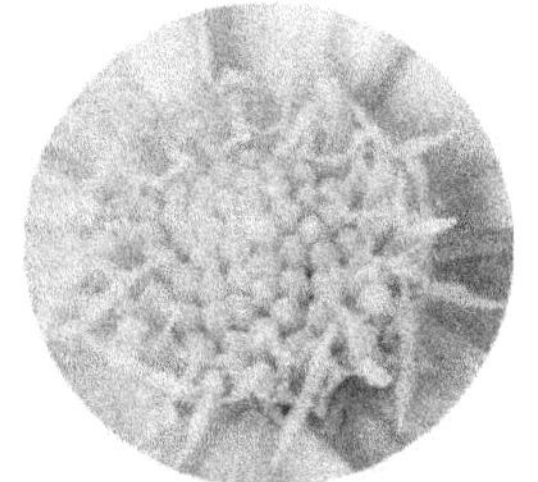

dahlia flower

Two Truths and a FIB about...

Vermeer

She pours one cup of milk,
to make a loaf of bread.
Light shines through the window
on the white cap on her head.

©2023, Linda A. Dryfhout

Footnote: **The Milkmaid** is an oil-on-canvas painting of a "milkmaid" hanging in the Rijksmuseum in Amsterdam, the Netherlands.

Landscape dotted with
windmills turning in the wind.
This is where I live.

© 2023, Linda A. Dryfhout

I

am

known as

painter of

light and have painted

one hundred pieces of artwork.

©2023, Linda A. Dryfhout

Vermeer painted less than 100 paintings in his lifetime. Some art scholars say 34 of his paintings have survived. Others say maybe 36.

Poetry Forms:

Truth #1: **Quatrain**

- has a four-line stanza
- in this poem the second and fourth lines rhyme
- in some quatrains the first two lines and last two lines rhyme or the first and third lines rhyme

Truth #2: **Haiku**

- a three line poem about nature
- the first line has five syllables
- the second line has seven syllables
- the third line has five syllables

Introducing the Poet...

# Linda A. Dryfhout

Linda A. Dryfhout loves being outside riding her bicycle. And she enjoys skydiving a few times each year. You can sometimes spot Linda practicing archery in her backyard.

Which statement about Linda is a FIB?
Turn to the "Poet Fact Check" section at the back of the book to find out!

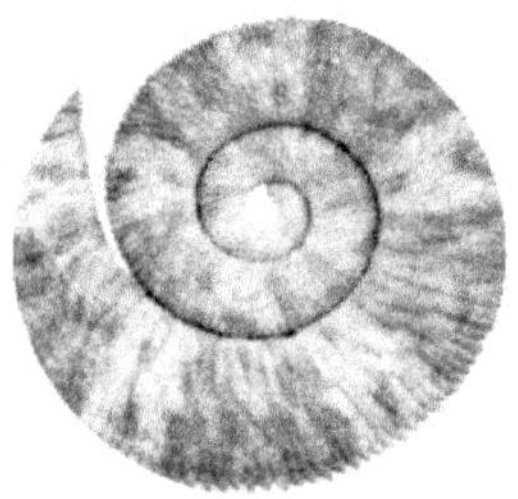

chamaeleo calyptratus tail

Two Truths and a FIB about...

Water

I like the sight of snow - on the mountains
Beauty in the shades of white
water - solidified
Not as solid as is ice
Tiny structured crystals - fractals
touching gently, holding hands
'til wind starts disuniting - spiraling
turning blue sky white
Slowly each one disappearing - to the eye
as the sun takes care of them
I'm cold but calm - seeing life so clearly now

©2023, Rolf A. Loch

World
Agitated -
Tranquility
Elicits
Reflections

©2023, Rolf A. Loch

Life
Death
Gentle
Powerful
Balancing extremes
Your softness is your greatest strength

Fact Check:

Using the unique properties of water as a metaphor for the unique properties of humans, the last sentence of this Fib. It is a myth that being vulnerable, empathetic and soft makes you weak. If used correctly, these qualities can be your greatest strength.

Poetry Forms:

Truth #1: **Freestyle Poem**

- based on a hike in the mountains where blowing snow inspired poem
- uses a reference to the mathematical concept of fractals
- uses a word game: the words behind the dash explain the main text and also form a new line/poem of itself, so a poem in a poem

Truth #2: **Acrostic**

- first letter in each line forms word, in this poem: WATER
- using water as a metaphor for self-reflection and meditation to stay calm in a stressed world: only calm water can reflect like a mirror

Introducing the Poet...

Rolf A. Loch

Rolf Loch, aka the Happy Healthy High-performer, helps people live more fulfilling lives as a health and performance coach, Mathematics and Physics teacher with a PhD in Physics, poet, songwriter and photographer. Early on he was inspired by Einstein's quote "the greatest scientists are artists as well". He wrote his first poem when he was still a baby.

Which statement about Rolf is a FIB?
Turn to the "Poet Fact Check" section at the back of the book to find out!

Chamomile flower

Poet Fact Check

"Math is the only place where truth and beauty mean the same thing."

Danica McKellar

Kathleen Mazurowski

William Peery

Margaret Simon

Colleen Murphy

Molly Hogan

Joan Riordan

Karuna Mistry

Linda Hofke

Mary Lee Hahn

Stephan Stücklin

Heidi Mordhorst

Cynthia L. Greene

Lill Pluta

Claire Schlinkert

Linda Baie

Carol Varsalona

Linda Mitchell

Tricia Torrible

Lisa Varchol Perron

Heather Kinser

Michelle Kogan

Rose Cappelli

Helen Kemp Zax

Kelly Conroy

Christy Mihaly

Jennifer Raudenbush

Molly Hogan

Karla Wendelin

Linda A. Dryfhout

Rolf A. Loch

nautilus sea shell

Introducing the Editor...

Bridget Magee

Bridget Magee and her nine brothers and sisters grew up in Southern California very near a Land with a grand castle housing various princesses, a huge rodent named Mickey, and a nightly firework show that she could see from her house. Now she lives in central Switzerland with her husband, Joe and jumpy dog, Smidgey, while her two daughters begin their adult lives in the United States. Nothing makes Bridget happier than a steaming cup of cappuccino (extra frothy) early in the morning.

Which statement about Bridget is a FIB? **Turn the page to find out!**

Bridget Magee

Want a to stay up-to-date on all things wee words for wee ones?

Email me at:

weewordsforweeones@gmail.com

Write "**Add me to your email list**" in the subject line and you will receive periodic emails announcing future anthology submission opportunities, book release information, book trailer videos, poetry, and the occasional message from my dog, Smidgey. You can unsubscribe at any time, I won't be offended. :)

Follow me:
Facebook: @weewordsforweeones
TikTok: @weewords